D0105211

WAKE UP, EMILY,
IT'S MOTHER'S DAY

OTHER YEARLING BOOKS BY
PATRICIA REILLY GIFF
(Illustrated by Blanche Sims)

The Kids of the Polk Street School books:

BEAST AND THE HALLOWEEN HORROR
LAZY LIONS, LUCKY LAMBS
SNAGGLE DOODLES
PURPLE CLIMBING DAYS
SAY "CHEESE"
SUNNY-SIDE UP
PICKLE PUSS
AND MORE

The Polka Dot Private Eye books:

THE MYSTERY OF THE BLUE RING
THE RIDDLE OF THE RED PURSE
THE SECRET AT THE POLK STREET SCHOOL
THE POWDER PUFF PUZZLE
THE CASE OF THE COOL-ITCH KID
GARBAGE JUICE FOR BREAKFAST
THE TRAIL OF THE SCREAMING TEENAGER
THE CLUE AT THE ZOO

YEARLING BOOKS/YOUNG YEARLINGS/YEARLING CLASSICS are designed especially to entertain and enlighten young people. Patricia Reilly Giff, consultant to this series, received her bachelor's degree from Marymount College and a master's degree in history from St. John's University. She holds a Professional Diploma in Reading and a Doctorate of Humane Letters from Hofstra University. She was a teacher and reading consultant for many years, and is the author of numerous books for young readers.

For a complete listing of all Yearling titles,
write to Dell Readers Service,
P.O. Box 1045, South Holland, IL 60473.

WAKE UP, EMILY, IT'S MOTHER'S DAY

Patricia Reilly Giff

Illustrated by Blanche Sims

A YEARLING BOOK

Published by
Dell Publishing
a division of
Bantam Doubleday Dell Publishing Group, Inc.
1540 Broadway
New York, New York 10036

ISBN: 0-440-40455-X

Printed in the United States of America

May 1991

10   9   8   7   6   5   4
OPM

For Jeremiah, Timothy, Terrance, and
Deirdre Gorman, Christopher Azzari,
Linsay Davis, Matthew La Pera, Leigh
Gorman, and Alicia and Mary Ann Quirk

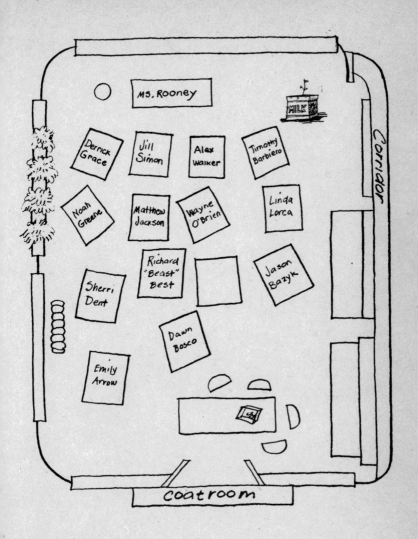

Chapter 1

Emily Arrow marched down the street. "Come on, Stacy," she told her little sister. "Let's move it."

Stacy moved like a snail. "I don't want to move it," she said. "I'm still tired."

Emily clicked her teeth.

Today was the worst day in the world.

Emily was wearing yesterday's jeans.

Her scribble-scrabble shirt was hanging out all over the place.

Her hair looked like the kitchen mop.

1

"I don't care," she told herself. "I don't care about one thing."

She hoped she wasn't going to cry.

She'd hate it if her eyes were all red.

Everyone in school would be asking what was wrong.

She kicked a stone out of her way.

This morning everyone in her house had overslept.

Her father had thrown the alarm clock in the garbage pail.

Her mother had yelled, "Hurry, hurry, eat, eat."

It wasn't Emily's fault that they had slept late.

Her mother hadn't even kissed her good-bye. She had raced off to her morning job.

Her father was still in the shower when Emily and Stacy had left for school.

"Wait up, guys," someone called.

It was Linda Lorca.

Emily turned.

Linda was out of breath. "A little late," she said. She waved her arm around. "Look what I have."

Emily looked. Linda was wearing a fat silver bracelet. It had a green diamond in the middle.

"It's a present I bought for my mother," Linda said. "You know, for a week from Sunday."

She smiled. "I sneaked it out. I wanted to give it a try."

She gave it a snap. "One size fits all."

"Gorgeous," said Emily.

Stacy skipped around them. "I don't like green, green, green," she sang under her breath.

Linda frowned. "Hey. I forgot something. My spelling homework."

Emily drew in her breath. "Hey," she said too.

She felt a lump of worry in her chest.

Stacy stopped skipping. "You didn't do your homework either, old Emily?"

Emily held up her hand. "Wait a minute."

Then she put her hand down. "Whew. I remember now. I did it right after school Friday."

"Good thing," Stacy said.

"Lucky," said Linda.

"Yes," said Emily.

They walked past Alex Walker's house.

His two-year-old brother, Donald, was running down the driveway.

Donald didn't have his shoes on. He didn't even have a shirt. His face was smeared with something purple.

Mrs. Walker was running after him.

Emily caught him before he reached the street.

"Thanks." Mrs. Walker pushed her hair off her forehead.

Emily rubbed her hands on her jeans.

Donald had gotten jelly all over her.

They watched Mrs. Walker carrying him inside.

A moment later Alex came tearing out of the house.

He was carrying a little bag in his hand.

He raced by them. "Got to play ball before the bell rings," he yelled.

Emily frowned.

There was something she should remember.

What was it? She shook her head.

They crossed the street and went inside the gates.

Emily felt messy, horrible.

"What's the matter with you anyway?" Linda asked.

Emily sighed. "Everything's wrong today. I'm a mess. My hair. Jelly all over me. And . . ."

She could see Alex playing ball.

He was playing with Beast and Matthew.

They were all in her special reading class.

Then she remembered.

"I forgot my reading homework for Mrs. Paris," she said. "I was supposed to bring dirt. Dirt in a Baggie. We're going to do something special today."

Emily headed for her classroom.

This was going to be the worst day of the whole year.

Chapter 2

A clock picture was pasted to Emily's desk.

It said 10:00.

All the special readers had clock pictures.

It told them when to go to Mrs. Paris's room.

Emily looked up at the wall clock.

Right now it was ten o'clock.

Beast stood up. So did Matthew and Alex.

They had Baggies of dirt in their hands.

Emily shoved her books into her desk.
She was last out the door.

Alex, Beast, and Matthew were hopping around in front of her.

Emily looked up at Mrs. Kara's bulletin board.

Mrs. Kara had started a new one.
It had a picture of a lady in the middle.
It had a big M on top.

Emily wondered what it was going to be.

She ran the eraser end of her pencil along the wall.

It left a little pink line.
She rubbed at it.

She wished she had remembered her dirt.

Beast turned around. "Hey, Emily Pemily, we're going to be late."

Emily raised one shoulder in the air.

The boys stopped.

"What's the matter?" Matthew asked.

"I forgot my dirt," Emily said.

"*Whoo-eee,*" said Beast. "You're going to be in trouble."

Emily nodded. "I know."

Matthew looked up at the ceiling. "I have an idea," he said. "The greatest idea in the world."

Emily leaned forward.

"We take a little dirt from my Baggie. We take some from Beast's . . ."

"And some from mine," Alex said.

Emily began to smile. "You saved my life," she said.

"I know," said Matthew.

Alex shook his head. "No, you didn't. How is Emily going to carry the dirt?"

No one said anything.

Then Beast started to laugh. "She could take off one shoe and . . ."

Alex and Matthew laughed too.

Emily felt like crying. "I'm in a lot of trouble, you know."

They stopped laughing.

"I know," said Matthew. "Wait right here."

He raced back to Ms. Rooney's room.

He was out the door a minute later. He waved his lunch box in the air.

He knelt down on the floor and opened it.

Inside was a tuna fish sandwich and a banana.

"Don't need the tuna fish Baggie," he said.

He pulled the sandwich out of the Baggie, took a bite, and put the sandwich back in the lunch box.

"Here you are, Emily," he said. "One Baggie." He sniffed. "Smells a little fishy."

"So what," Emily said. "You really did save my life."

They stood in a circle.

The boys poured dirt into the Baggie.

"Watch out," said Matthew. "It's all over the floor."

Mrs. Kettle came down the hall.

She was the strictest teacher in the whole school.

"Good grief," she said. "What kind of a mess are you making?"

"Dirt dessert," said Matthew.

Mrs. Kettle stared at him. "You are not funny, young man. Not one bit . . ."

Emily rubbed at the dirt with her foot.

Mrs. Kettle turned to look at Emily. "I think you're scratching the floor, young lady."

Emily stopped rubbing. "I'm sorry," she said. "Really sorry."

"You'd better get where you're going," said Mrs. Kettle. "Stop dropping dirt. I'll get this mess cleaned up."

Emily and the boys quick-stepped down the hall to Room 100.

Mrs. Paris was waiting for them. "I thought you'd never get here," she said. "I've been waiting."

Emily looked at the boys.

Matthew rolled his eyes a little.

Then they sat down at the round reading table.

"Did everyone remember to bring soil Baggies?" Mrs. Paris asked.

They held them up in the air.

Emily smiled at the boys.

Then she leaned forward.

She couldn't wait to find out what this dirt business was all about.

Chapter 3

"Do you know what today is?" Mrs. Paris asked.

"It's not my birthday," said Beast.

"Not mine either," said Matthew.

Emily tried to think.

It was just a plain old Monday.

Mrs. Paris took a piece of pink chalk. She drew a flower on the chalkboard. "It's May first," she said.

Emily frowned. "I didn't hear any firecrackers."

Beast began to laugh. He gave Emily a little punch. "That's Fourth of July."

Emily felt her cheeks get hot. "I forgot," she said.

Mrs. Paris shook her head at Beast. "We all forget sometimes," she said.

Emily looked up at Mrs. Paris.

Mrs. Paris was old.

She had eyeglasses and a bunch of wrinkles.

She was the nicest teacher Emily knew.

Mrs. Paris nodded.

"May is an interesting month," she said. "In the olden days people thought there was a goddess named Flora. They thought Flora made the flowers grow. Every year they had a party for her."

Emily looked out the window.

The grass was beginning to grow.

Green spots were poking up out of the brown.

16

Mrs. Paris gave everyone a sheet of paper. "Can you read what this says?"

Emily looked down at her paper.

The top part was easy.

MAKE THE EARTH BEAUTIFUL.

The next line had two words.

The first word was GROWING.

She knew that one.

She spelled the second word. "M-a-r-i-g-o-l-d-s."

That was too hard for her.

It was too hard for Beast too.

She could hear him trying to sound it out.

Mrs. Paris put four milk containers on the table.

"Flowerpots," she said.

Emily picked one up.

It still smelled like milk.

"Whew." Beast wrinkled his nose. "This smells gross."

"Don't worry," said Mrs. Paris. "We'll wash them out."

Mrs. Paris sat down at the table. "Well?" she asked. "Who can tell us . . ."

Emily looked down at her paper.

She hoped Mrs. Paris wouldn't call on her.

She looked at that second word again. MARIGOLDS.

"Hey," she said. "The end part is *gold*."

"Wonderful," said Mrs. Paris.

Emily looked at the first part again.

"I'll give you a hint," said Mrs. Paris. "You know those orange flowers . . ."

"Marigolds," said Emily. "GROWING MARIGOLDS."

19

Alex slid down in his chair. "I thought we were going to make something good. Something like machines."

"*Vroom, vroom,*" said Matthew.

Mrs. Paris smiled. "Who knows what else happens this month?"

"Easy," said Alex.

"Double easy," said Matthew.

"Yes," said Emily. She tried to think as fast as she could.

Mrs. Paris smiled harder. "I think you're all teasing me. I don't think you know."

Alex ducked his head.

Then Matthew started to laugh.

Emily laughed too.

"Wake up," said Mrs. Paris. "It's Mother's Day."

"Hey, that's right," Beast said.

Emily sat back. Of course. Mrs. Kara's

bulletin board.

M was for *mother*.

She nodded to herself.

Linda was giving her mother a bracelet for Mother's Day.

"Yes," said Mrs. Paris. "Mother's Day is in less than two weeks."

"*Whoo-eee,*" said Beast. "I have to get my mother a present."

"I was thinking," Mrs. Paris said. "Thinking about Flora, and pretty flowers. I was thinking about making the earth beautiful."

"I was thinking about that too," Emily said, fingers crossed. She always wanted Mrs. Paris to think she was a great kid.

Mrs. Paris nodded at her. "We could make the earth beautiful by growing marigolds."

"In stinky flowerpots that smell like milk?" Alex said.

Alex was fresh today, Emily thought. Very fresh.

Mrs. Paris didn't look at Alex. She kept talking. "At the same time we can give our mothers Mother's Day presents. I have a package of marigold seeds right here."

Emily looked at the milk containers.

Alex was right.

It would be a stinky present.

She'd never tell Mrs. Paris that though.

She went with the boys to wash out the milk containers.

She'd have to think of something for her mother.

Something much better than marigolds in a milky milk container.

Chapter 4

It was Friday.

School was over for the week.

Emily and Stacy walked home to-gether.

Stacy was carrying a rolled-up paper.

It was almost as big as she was.

It was the Mother's Day card she had made in school.

Alex Walker's father waved at them. He was working in his garden.

"I'm planting dahlias," he said.

Emily thought about Mrs. Paris.

"You're making the earth beautiful," she said.

"Exactly right," said Mr. Walker.

"Exactly right," said Stacy as they turned the corner. She began to sing. "Gor-ge-us is my presss-sssent."

Emily shook her head. "Could you stop singing for a minute? I'm trying to think."

Stacy stopped. "Too bad you can't think while I sing."

"Mmm," Emily said. She was thinking about school.

Everyone was making the earth beautiful.

Some classes had flower pictures pasted on their windows.

Ms. Rooney had a red rose tacked to the door of Room 113.

Drake Evan's class was planting a garden in the school yard.

And something else.

Alex, Beast, and Matthew had tiny green shoots in their milk containers.

Not Emily though.

All she had was a pack of dirt in an old milk container.

"Don't worry," Mrs. Paris had said. "It will grow in its own good time."

It wasn't growing.

Not even a speck.

Emily had stuck her finger in the milk container this morning.

She had rooted around until she found the seed.

It was long. It was black on one end. It had a little tan tassel on the other end.

Nothing seemed to be happening to it.

Emily had stuck it back in the container.

Maybe it would grow tonight.

Right now Emily followed Stacy into the house.

"Shhh," Stacy said. "Don't let anyone hear us."

"Don't worry." Emily could hear their mother in the laundry room. The washing machine was swishing. The dryer door banged shut.

Stacy and Emily tiptoed up the stairs.

None of the beds were made today.

They had overslept again.

They didn't have an alarm clock to wake them up.

Everyone had to race out of the house this morning in two minutes.

"Into the closet with this baby." Stacy held up her Mother's Day card. "It's the best one in the world," she said. "I'm going to show it to Daddy when he gets home."

Emily smiled.

What a mess Stacy's Mother's Day card was.

It was a picture of her mother.

She had a huge smile.

She had about a hundred pointy little teeth.

"Is that you, girls?" their mother called from downstairs.

"Me and Emily," said Stacy. "Doing secret things."

"I have a secret snack downstairs," their mother called back. "It's delicious."

Stacy slammed the closet door shut tight.

She reached for a piece of paper.

ST OT

"Stay out," she said. She put the sign

in front of the door. "So Mommy doesn't see her present."

Stacy pulled off her sweater. "What are you giving Mommy anyway?" she asked.

Emily looked out the window. "It's a secret."

"A good secret?" Stacy asked. "As good as mine?"

Emily sighed. "No. It's not really a secret. I don't know what to get her yet."

"Eddie is giving his mother candy," said Stacy. "He ate a piece though. He's trying not to eat another one."

Emily laughed.

Together they went downstairs.

On the table was a plate of apple slices.

A hill of raisins was piled in the middle.

"You're the best mother," Stacy said.

Emily looked up at her mother.

Mrs. Arrow had straight brown hair like Emily's.

She had a pointy chin like Stacy's.

Stacy was right, Emily thought.

She was the best mother in the world.

She had to get her a terrific present for Mother's Day.

She popped an apple slice into her mouth.

"If you had a wish," she asked her mother, "what would you want for Mother's Day?"

Mrs. Arrow looked up at the ceiling. "Someone to set the table every night for a week?"

"Not like that," Emily said. "Something real."

Mrs. Arrow sighed. "I don't need

something real. I need ten minutes to put my feet up."

Emily shook her head. "That's not a good present."

Emily picked up a magazine next to her.

The front cover showed a lady standing on the lawn.

She had on a sparkly necklace.

Emily started to page through the magazine.

Then she had an idea.

A wonderful idea.

The best Mother's Day idea in the world.

Chapter 5

Emily was early for school on Monday.

Still she had to hurry.

She was dying to talk with Linda Lorca.

She stopped at the gates to catch her breath.

Across the yard the girls were playing double-dutch jump rope.

The boys were playing Got You Last.

"Come on, Emily," Jill Simon called. "We need you to turn."

Emily waved. "One minute, all right?"

She looked around.

She couldn't see Linda anywhere.

Then she spotted her.

Linda was heading for the big brown doors into school.

"Wait," she yelled.

Linda turned.

"Can't," she said. "I'm dying of thirst."

Emily ran to catch up.

The sixth-grade monitor blew her whistle. "No running in the school yard," she shouted.

Emily slowed down.

Linda slowed down too.

They climbed the steps.

"No going inside before the bell," the monitor said.

Emily made a face.

It was the mean monitor, the one with the fat cheeks and the ponytail.

The monitor put her hands on her hips. "No making faces either."

Emily and Linda backed down the steps.

They walked around the side of the building.

Emily looked over her shoulder.

The monitor was blowing her whistle at someone. It was a girl hopping around the dumpster.

"Quick," Emily said.

They ducked in the side door.

"Safe," said Linda.

"Listen," Emily said. "I have to ask you something."

Linda headed for the water fountain. "What?"

"It's about your bracelet," Emily said.

Linda bent over and took a drink. *"Gfft sptt,"* she said.

She waved one arm in the air.

Emily could see she was wearing a little silver bracelet.

"Not that one," she said.

Just then Mrs. Paris went by. "Good morning, girls," she said. "How would you like to toss these papers in my room?"

Linda stood up. "Sure," they both said at once.

Emily bent over the fountain quickly. The water was cold on her teeth. Icy. Then she straightened up.

She and Linda took the papers from Mrs. Paris.

Mrs. Paris opened the door to the teacher's room. "This gives me time for a quick cup of coffee," she said.

"You were asking me . . ." Linda said to Emily.

"Your mother's bracelet," Emily said, "the one-size-fits-all—"

"Sure," said Linda. She frowned. "The one I broke over the weekend."

Emily nodded. "I guess so."

"Snapped the thing in half," said Linda. "Now I have to buy another one."

"How about I go with you?" Emily said. "I'll buy one for my mother too."

"Sure. At Gracie's Gifts," Linda said.

Emily put the papers on Mrs. Paris's desk. She hoped she had enough birthday money left in her bank. "How much?" she asked.

"Two dollars. We could go next Saturday."

"Great." Emily took a breath. "Terrific." She probably had enough.

"Hey," said Linda. "What's that

stuff?'' She pointed to the milk containers on Mrs. Paris's windowsill.

''Marigolds,'' said Emily.

She could see little green leaves on everyone's plants.

Everyone but hers.

Linda walked over to the window. ''Which one is . . .''

''The plain brown dirt one,'' said Emily. ''No leaves, no flowers, no nothing.''

Carefully Linda lifted it up.

She closed one eye and squinted at it. ''Not enough water.''

''Really?''

''You've got to dump in a whole pile.''

Emily poked her finger in. ''You're right,'' she said. ''It is a little crumbly.''

She picked up Mrs. Paris's green watering can. She didn't stop pouring until the top was soaked.

"One more squirt," said Linda. "For luck."

Emily poured in a little more.

"Looks as if this will be a swimming marigold."

She smiled.

Maybe Linda had solved all her problems.

She crossed her fingers.

She hoped so.

Chapter 6

It was Friday, two more days until Mother's Day.

Emily followed Alex, Beast, and Matthew down the hall.

It was a no-reading day in Mrs. Paris's room.

Instead they were going to decorate their milk containers.

At the same time Mrs. Paris was going to read to them. "Listening to a story counts too," she always said.

Mrs. Paris was waiting for them.

She had a sheet of pink cellophane paper for Emily.

She had yellow ones for the boys.

She had rolls of ribbon too . . . white, and blue, and green.

She handed out the milk containers.

"Oh, dear," she said when she saw Emily's. "I think this poor thing is drowning."

Beast stood up to take a look. *"Glub, blub,"* he said.

Emily swallowed.

Muddy water floated on top of her container.

The whole thing was a mess.

"You didn't make the earth very beautiful," said Alex. He started to laugh.

Mrs. Paris patted Emily on the shoulder. "I wish I had more marigold seed," she said. "I wish Mother's Day weren't coming in two days."

Emily tried to look as if she didn't care.

"Wrap it up anyway," said Matthew. "Your mother won't mind."

"Besides," Beast said. "It might start to grow over the weekend."

Mrs. Paris nodded slowly. "I'll tell you what, Emily. Let's get rid of some of this water. We'll wrap it up nicely. I'll bring more seed on Monday. Tell your mother we'll give it another try next week."

"I'm going to get my mother something else anyway," Emily said.

She looked down at the milk container.

Alex was right. She wasn't making the earth beautiful.

It would have been nice to give her mother a marigold along with the bracelet.

Suddenly she remembered that her mother liked flowers.

She hoped she wasn't going to cry.

Just then Mrs. Zachary stuck her head in the door.

"Help," she said to Mrs. Paris. "I need to see Emily Arrow. Right this second."

Mrs. Paris gave Emily another pat on the shoulder. "I'll wrap this for you, Emily," she said. "I'll make it as pretty as I can."

"You saved my life," Mrs. Zachary said to Mrs. Paris.

She looked at Emily.

"Will you come down to my room? Poor Stacy is going to flood my room with tears."

Emily drew in her breath. "What's the matter?"

"I don't know," said Mrs. Zachary. "I was counting snack money. All of a sudden Stacy started to cry."

Mrs. Zachary raised her shoulders in the air. "I want to make her feel better. But she won't tell me what happened."

They hurried down the hall.

Emily could hear Mrs. Zachary's class.

They were talking and running around.

She could hear Stacy too.

Stacy was crying.

Howling.

She sounded like Elwood, the dog down the street.

Emily rubbed her hands on her jeans.

Then she dashed in the door.

"What's the matter, Stacy?" she asked.

Stacy didn't answer though.

She just kept crying.

Chapter 7

Emily opened her eyes.

She didn't have to worry about being on time today.

It was Saturday.

She climbed out of bed and went over to the window.

Her marigold plant was hidden behind the curtain.

Pretty pink cellophane swirled around it.

A blue ribbon held it all together.

Outside in the yard everything was growing.

Emily could see that the grass was greener. A yellow flower had popped up near the fence.

Inside, things weren't as good.

The dirt in the marigold pot was brown and wet.

In the other bed Stacy turned over.

Emily sighed.

Poor Stacy had cried for an hour yesterday.

She had cried so loud, Emily's ears were ringing.

It was all because of Patty and Eddie and Annie in Stacy's class.

For Mother's Day Eddie was giving his mother candy.

Patty had a picture for her mother.

And Annie had a handkerchief for hers.

"What good is a card?" Eddie had

asked Stacy. "You can't eat it. You can't use it for anything."

"That's right," Patty said. "It's good for nothing."

And Annie had laughed.

"A big *ha-ha* laugh," Stacy had told Emily.

"I need a present," Stacy had whispered. "A good present. And I don't have any money."

Emily looked out the window for another minute.

She was going to help Stacy.

She knew just how to do it.

She went over to her dresser.

Her pink piggy bank was in the top drawer.

Emily sank down on the floor with it.

She shook it over the rug.

A couple of pennies clinked out.

They rolled under her bed.

Emily held up the bank. She looked into the slit in the pig's head with one eye.

Snaggle doodles.

This was going to take a long time.

She could see her folded dollars way back.

She was saving them for a wedding dress when she grew up.

She'd have to worry about the dress next year.

She shook the bank again.

This time a quarter rolled out.

"Good," she said. She shook it back and forth as hard as she could.

"Not good," said Stacy. "You're making a ton of noise."

Emily smiled over at her. "I have an idea," she said.

Stacy sat up in bed. She yawned. "What, old Emily?"

"You and I are going to get dressed. Right this minute. We're . . ."

"Emily," a voice screeched. "Emmmmm-ly Arrow."

"Who's that?" Stacy asked. "Making all that noise."

Emily poked her head out the window.

Linda Lorca was outside.

She was wearing a yellow raincoat.

She had a huge plastic bag under one arm.

"I'll be down in two minutes." Emily tried to say it in a whisper.

She shook the piggy bank again.

She reached for the edge of the bills and yanked.

There. A couple of dollars. She had enough.

She raced over to her closet.

She pulled her old pink party dress over her head.

She kicked her red sneakers out from under her bed.

"Get up, Stacy," she said. "Throw on your clothes. We've got things to do today."

Chapter 8

"All the way to Gracie's Gifts?" their mother asked. "Why?"

"I don't know," said Stacy.

Emily shook her head. "It's a surprise."

Mrs. Arrow's forehead wrinkled. "You have to be careful. Very careful. Hold hands crossing the street."

"Don't worry." Emily pulled on her red jacket. "I'll be careful as anything."

"Emily," Linda screeched from outside.

Emily clicked her teeth. "Coming,"

she screeched back. "Coming right now."

She and Stacy banged out the door.

Linda was sitting on the curb. Her yellow rain hood was pulled up over her head.

Stacy held out her hand. "I don't feel any drops. It's sunny out."

Linda turned. "I've been waiting all this time—" She broke off.

She looked at Stacy. "It's a long, long way to Gracie's Gifts."

She patted her pack. "I took everything. Just in case. Raincoat if it rains. A bottle of water. Half a butterscotch bar . . ."

They started down the street.

Stacy wasn't such a hot walker, Emily thought. Maybe she shouldn't have let her come.

They turned the corner.

Alex Walker's little brother, Donald, was running down the street.

He had on almost no clothes.

A diaper. One sock. A shoe.

He was covered with chocolate.

Mrs. Walker raced down her driveway. "Catch that kid," she called.

Emily reached out.

He darted past her.

He left a chocolate streak across her jacket.

Stacy reached out too. "Gooey. Ugh," she said. She grabbed the top of his diaper.

"Thanks." Mrs. Walker smiled at them. She put Donald over her shoulder. She marched back toward her house.

Emily looked at her sleeve. "Yucks."

She had to take Stacy's hand to cross the street.

Stacy was as sticky as she was.

And Stacy was getting tired. "I have to sit down," she said.

Linda put her hands on her hips. "This isn't supposed to take all day, you know."

Stacy stuck out her lip. "My feet hurt. My bones hurt."

Emily patted Stacy's back. "Just a little more."

They started up again.

Linda was chewing on her butter-scotch bar.

It was a good thing Stacy hated butterscotch, Emily thought. Linda hadn't even given them a sniff.

Even so, Stacy was ready to cry.

She was getting cranky. Very cranky.

Emily swallowed. She was dying for a drink of water. "How about a sip of water?" she asked Linda.

Linda thought for a moment. "I don't have that much," she said.

It seemed to take forever to get there. At last Emily could see the big street. She could see the sign on the corner:

GREAT GIFTS AT GRACIE'S

Linda wiped her mouth. She pointed. "Here we are."

They raced toward the door.

"Are we buying me something?" Stacy asked.

Emily stopped.

She couldn't believe it.

She had forgotten to tell Stacy what this was all about.

She smiled. "Good news, Stacy," she said. "We're buying Mother a present. Together. You and me. For Mother's Day."

Stacy began to smile "Great idea," she sang. "Great, great, great."

Emily pointed to the window. "Look."

A row of bracelets was lined up in front.

Beautiful bracelets with little green stones.

"Those?" Stacy frowned a little. "Not too good. I don't like green."

Then she smiled. "I see something, old Emily. I see the perfect present for Mommy. You have to buy it."

Emily looked to where Stacy was pointing.

She began to shake her head. It was a terrible Mother's Day present, she thought.

But Stacy's eyes were shining. "That's it, old Emily," she said. "It's just perfect, isn't it?"

Chapter 9

Emily opened her eyes.

It was early, very early.

She could hear a robin outside.

Everything else was quiet.

Stacy was a lump under the covers.

Her mother and father must still be asleep too.

Then Emily remembered. It was Mother's Day.

Her poor mother.

Gracie had wrapped their gift in pink and green.

She had put on a special bow.

Emily shook her head.

Wait till her mother saw it.

A stinky gray alarm clock.

Stacy loved it.

"We'll never be late again," she said.

Emily looked out the window.

It was pretty outside. More flowers were beginning to bloom.

Someday she was going to buy her mother that bracelet.

A hundred bracelets.

When she was rich. If she ever was rich.

She was going to make sure her mother never had to work so hard either.

Maybe she could do something right now.

Emily put on her robe.

She tiptoed downstairs.

What could she do?

She could get breakfast for her mother.

Breakfast in bed.

She worked quickly.

She put cereal in a bowl . . . and milk and sugar on a tray.

Her father came into the kitchen.

He was yawning.

"You're up early," he said smiling.

Emily nodded. "It's Mother's Day."

Her father nodded too. "Breakfast in bed for Mom?"

"Yes. I'm going to make toast in a minute."

"Great idea," her father said. "I'll make the coffee."

Emily took a small glass out of the closet. She poured in orange juice.

She put bread into the toaster.

Then she looked at the tray.

It looked terrific.

A speck of milk had dripped on the pink paper napkin.

Her mother would never see it though.

Her father put his hand on her head.

"She'll know how much you love her when she sees this."

Emily nodded. "I guess so."

She felt a little better.

But not perfect.

"Wait a minute," she told her father. "I'll go wake Stacy."

He smiled. "It'll take ten for the coffee. I'll bring up the tray."

Emily tiptoed up the stairs.

She went past her mother's room.

Her mother was still asleep.

Stacy was awake though.

She was standing next to the window.

She was holding the alarm-clock present.

"Mommy's going to love this," she said.

Emily nodded.

Stacy pointed to the windowsill. "She's going to love something else too."

Emily looked.

She looked hard.

Coming up in the marigold container was a tiny shoot of green.

You could hardly see it.

But it was there.

She'd put it on the breakfast tray.

She smiled. She was helping to make the earth beautiful.

Her mother would love it.

Emily could smell the coffee downstairs. "Come on, Stacy," she said.

She could hear her father coming with the breakfast tray.

"Wake up," she called to her mother. "It's Mother's Day."